Forever
And
Always

To a great friend
Mark Haase,

Christy Smith

Christy Smith

Forever and Always

Forever and Always

This novel is a work of fiction. Names, characters, places and incidents
either are the product of the author's imagination or are used
fictitiously. Any resemblance to actual events, locales, organizations or
persons living or dead is entirely coincidental.

Whosoever Press books may be ordered through booksellers or by
contacting: Whosoever Press
        P.O. Box 1513
        Boaz, AL 35957
        www.whosoeverpress.com
        1-256-706-3315

Because of the dynamic nature of the Internet, any web addresses or
links contained in this book may have changed since publication and
may no longer be valid. The views expressed in this work are solely
those of the author and do not necessarily reflect the views of the
publisher, and the publisher hereby disclaims any responsibility for
them.

Any people depicted in stock imagery provided by Thinkstock are
models, and such images are being used for illustrative purposes only.

Certain stock imagery © Thinkstock.
ISBN-10: 0615755526 (sc)
ISBN-13: 978-0615755526 (sc)
ISBN: 978-1-4497-3525-8 (e)

Library of Congress Control Number: 2011963160

Printed in the United States of America

Whosoever Press rev. date: 3/15/2013

Dedication

To God, to whom I give all praise and thanksgiving. May this book bring you praise and glory.

To Jerry, my best friend, and wonderful husband. You are my everything.

To my maternal grandparents, Harold and Ruth for their eternal belief in me.

To Mom and Dad, for teaching me about unconditional love by example.

To Carolyn, thank you for being you.

Forever and Always

~

Forever and Always provides the reader with the ups and downs of the freshly discovered love of a young couple, Patricia Heifelmeyer and John McDougal, at the end of the Civil War. The location of the book is Orleans Parish, the year of our Lord 1864. The war is almost over.

Love, laughter, learning, mystery, secrecy, and murder are all woven through the pages of this book. The American Civil War raged from 1861 until 1865 and claimed more than 600,000 lives. Is John McDougal among their number?

Table of Contents

Forever and Always,
Orleans Parish, the year of our Lord 1864

Chapter 1

Memories and a Guest

The Heifelmeyers had risen in wealth and prominence in 1852 by benefit of Margaret's family. Patricia Heifelmeyer was fourteen years old, the daughter of a proper English mother, Margaret, and a very rigid German father. When Klaus Heifelmeyer was home, he told Margaret and Patricia, "I'm working. Leave me alone. I am not to be disturbed for any reason," as the study door closed.

Margaret would gather courage to knock on the door, "Klaus, Cook has lunch ready." She was met with protest for any interruption. Business meetings were always

1

secret, since Klaus was one of the heads of the Underground Railroad in the area. Klaus spent most of his time "out in the field" dealing with any problems and making sure the slaves were being treated fairly.

Margaret, pulled up her long, brown hair and worked it into a different style each day. If her dress soiled, even a little, she was off to change. Her speech was precise, her manners genteel. She was always immaculate and very proper, and she tried to raise Patricia the same.

Her father, Klaus, on the other hand, was quite businesslike; his mind was always on his work in the Underground Railroad. Being a station master, he was fully dedicated to the cause; it consumed him. Keeping his involvement from everyone a secret had taken an emotional toll on him. Under the estate, Klaus had rooms constructed for those slaves who were too scared to stay in the barn. They were better accommodations than slaves were used to, especially those escaping from their masters.

Sometimes a girl just needs to speak to her father, but most times, he was unavailable to her, either shut in the study or out in the field, making sure things went well. When she did get the chance to speak to him, she felt hurried because he wanted to get back to his business dealings. Patricia knew that he loved her; he just had difficulty showing it.

(Patricia's family upbringing instilled in her a healthy respect for elders. All were addressed formally, especially her parents). Patricia was quite close to her mother. They spent quite a lot of time reading, talking, and doing needlework in each other's company. Truth be known, Patricia adored her mother. She sorely missed the time they used to spend together preparing meals. She loved learning about baking. Since they moved to the estate and employed the servants, they did not do that much anymore. When they did, it was a real treat for both. Father kept saying, "We have come up in society now, and that's what he hired Cook for!" Klaus did not realize how much both Patricia and her mother enjoyed baking and preparing meals. Every so often, they would do some baking anyway and swear cook to secrecy, which made those times even more special.

In the last three years, the family had become very prominent. They had moved to the estate in the past year. They now owned a great expanse of land. To Patricia, it seemed as if their property was endless. Sometimes she missed the old house, the time before the family's wealth. Life may have been harder, but it was satisfying to work in the fields as they used to. Now with all the servants and farmhands, sometimes it was hard to stay occupied.

I do still have my reading and needlework, she thought. She had been doing needlework two hours a day for years now. Mother insisted on that. Her needlework lessons had begun at age eight. In the beginning, she was given scraps of material to work with. Mother had been very stern about the way to hold things and that the stitches were correctly done and of uniform length. After trying repeatedly, she began to win Mother's praise. A word of praise and her eyes shone brightly, and she was determined to do even better. The designs became more difficult, but Patricia would not be discouraged. The harder the work, the more she tried, not just to please Mother, but for her own satisfaction.

Patricia's thirst for knowledge was intense. She did not really care what the subject; she just loved to read. Given a choice, her favorite would be poetry. Patricia's manners were exquisitely honed except for an occasional outburst, usually of laughter, which her mother tried desperately to control.

She was a happy child. Often, Mother would smile broadly—privately, of course.

Public shows of emotion were unthinkable. Even so, sometimes it was quite difficult for Mother to maintain control. Patricia did many things that brought back memories of her own childhood and the difficult times her own mother had in raising her. Margaret vowed never to let Patricia know how carefree she was as a child. She had become so different with the responsibilities of adulthood and marriage to Patricia's father.

Fourteen was such an awkward age. Still more child than woman physically, Patricia was facing a constant war of emotions. She had grown to be a beautiful woman-child. Mother knew it would not be long before many suitors would begin to appear, and she held conflicting emotions when it came to Patricia's coming womanhood. She feared for her, yet she was ecstatic for her too, knowing of the exciting times close on the horizon for Patricia.

Patricia was particularly fond of the stable. She loved the smell of the hay and talking to the horses. Jasper, the stable keeper, and she had become as close as acceptable for someone in her position. They both enjoyed the few conversations they'd had.

Although he actually had no right at twenty-eight and in his position, Jasper found himself looking out for Patricia more as she was coming of age. He felt somewhat responsible for her safety.

Even though Klaus agreed with the North on the issue of slavery, they lived in New Orleans, so he had to keep up the ruse of being an uncaring slave owner to the townspeople and for the sake of his "slaves." He was against restraining another human being for the good of another, no matter what race was involved. He was a good Christian man, and he felt that keeping someone against his or her will was just wrong. In the Holy Bible, as God speaks to Moses, He says He heard the cries of His people. In Exodus 3:10, from the burning bush, God says, "I am sending you to Pharaoh to bring my people the Israelites out of Egypt." No good Christian would go against the Bible. Klaus had become a part of the Underground Railroad as soon as he discovered it existed and continued to be kind to his slaves.

Father put up a notice today for an overseer. The family already had slaves; the work was long and strenuous. Patricia saw very little of the slaves. They arrived before daybreak, worked through the day, and returned to their families at night. All but Jasper lived on the other side of the creek in a communal arrangement. Klaus allowed Jasper to stay in the barn so he could tend to the animals when needed.

Patricia was a slender girl with blue eyes that shone like the most beautiful sky you would ever see. Her hair was golden blonde, reaching midway down her back. She was a lovely young girl. At this time in her life, she was confused. Changes were taking place, both physically and mentally.

That evening at suppertime, there was a knock on the door. As Patricia opened the door, in walked a man none of them had ever seen before. "The name is John McDougal. I was passing through town and saw your notice. Might I be of some help?" Father extended his hand, and the man greeted him with a hearty handshake.

Klaus hired Mr. McDougal on the spot because of that handshake, Patricia later learned. Father always did think that you could tell the kind of man you were dealing with by his handshake. Father explained that he was to be the permanent overseer. He would stay on the property in the shack down by the creek. Father wanted him available at a moment's notice. He was to move into the shack as soon as possible.

John stood tall; with his broad shoulders and lean waist, he would make an excellent farmhand. He would be able to do much of the heavy work that was necessary on the estate.

John McDougal's sole intention as he had come up to the door that first evening was to get a job. He was a traveler and man of the world. He had lost his virginity at the young age of twelve to the wife of a former employer. The farmer's wife had cornered him in the hayloft in the barn. "Either you do, or I'll tell my husband that you did!" Because of his age, John was unaware of what to do. The farmer's wife eagerly showed the boy how to proceed.

Throughout his travels, John had been with many a farmer's daughter. That night, when he came to the Heifelmeyers' front door, he noted Patricia when she answered the door with a heavy sigh and a look that went from his eyes to his manhood. *She is just another farmer's daughter just like all the others I've encountered*, he thought. Though he knew at first glance that she was a young one, he mentally filed that information away for possible later use.

Patricia, upon opening the door, felt as if she'd been hit in the forehead with a thunderbolt. Every sense in her seemed to wake up. Patricia noticed immediately that John was unique. Instantly she became aware of his full, thick, black hair and brown eyes.

8

His eyes seem to sparkle, or is that my imagination? Their eyes met just briefly, acknowledging each other as something deep within her stirred. I like the twinkle in his eyes. Who is this man that awoke these strange sensations in me?

As the days progressed, John proved himself to be quite an excellent overseer. *Am I mistaken or is Father testing this new overseer more than the others?* The question crossed Patricia's mind in a flash and was immediately dismissed, or so she thought. The tasks John was given—and their number was quite large—were done cheerily, and Father was well pleased.

John began watching Patricia on the first day of his employment. *Is this farmer's daughter like all the others?* Not allowed in the house, his view of her was somewhat limited. She came outside each morning very early, seeming not to notice anyone or anything. She seemed to drink in the sunshine as it rose in all of its glory. *She almost dances in its warmth;* he thought, *Her long, blonde hair swaying back and forth as she lets the warmth envelop her.* Again, John noticed her youthfulness.

Often she would wander to her favorite spot on the grounds. Easily overlooked was a small stream to the east of her favorite tree, with an omnipresent flow of water trickling through the rocks. Its waters were clear and cool as a late October sky. Her mind whirling, she would settle herself beneath her special tree, lean back, close her eyes, and try to understand. Questions kept nagging at her. Why did her breasts hurt so? Why did her heart ache one moment and race like her father's fastest horse the next? So many questions! She wanted to approach her mother for help, but she just did not know how. She wasn't afraid to approach her, just hesitant; but she wasn't always in this frame of mind. Usually she was quite happy. And this place! It held such happiness and a sense of security for Patricia. This was the one place she could come to work out her problems, treasure her secrets, do some thinking, and best of all, the one place where she could relax and be herself. She could do what she wanted here, and she did! She read, wrote, wondered, yes, even sang and laughed here.

Chapter 2

The Growing Years

Time passed quickly. Patricia mused,
It has been good to spend time with the horses
again. I enjoy spending time with Jasper too.
He knows so much about horses. He always
teaches me so much. Jasper liked her too, for
her interest in his knowledge, her love for the
horses, and her ability to talk to them. Why
doesn't Mother like me spending time in the
stable? I just love the book Father gave me as
a birthday gift. She read the inscription again,
"To my daughter Patricia, on the occasion of
her fifteenth birthday. Father." It wasn't just
any book, however. It was her very own copy
of Poems by John Keats, her favorite poet.

She was on her way now, book and
daisy in hand, to her special spot on the
grounds, her special tree, wanting to drink in
every last word of that book. Hearing the
sounds of wood being chopped and knowing
John was close by comforted her.

Engrossed in her book, Patricia didn't
see him pass with the fresh-cut wood. John

finished stacking and watched her intently as he washed up in the trough.

On retiring to her room for the night, Patricia was surprised at what she found. Strewn about the open window, on the sill and the floor beneath were daises. Gathering them up, Patricia filled her tableside vase and arranged them in it. One from the sill fell back outside. Replacing the vase, she was still trying to figure out how they had gotten there. As she wondered, she took one and put it in her hair.

In the morning, the daisy was still in her hair, where it remained for the rest of the day. "Good morning, Miss Patricia."

"Good morning to you, John." The slightest smile crossed each of their faces. Patricia found herself reaching to touch the daisy every so often that day. It began to wilt from lack of water and excess of sun. To save it, Patricia pressed it in her book of poetry.

One late summer afternoon after Patricia's fifteenth birthday, she found herself out walking again, enjoying the sights and sounds of the oncoming autumn. Feeling the light breezes dancing in her hair, Patricia watched the new-fallen leaves racing across the meadow, hurrying to nowhere, took in the sweet, fresh scent of the air. *Autumn is a very busy, very alive time*; she thought. *It is my favorite time of the year.*

Walking and not paying particular attention to where she was going, she suddenly awoke from her own little world. She bumped into one of the trees in the meadow, landing abruptly on a clump of clover. Taken aback by the suddenness of it all, she sat there a moment, trying to catch her breath. Gathering herself, she heard something off in the distance that sounded like splashing. But it couldn't be; she was alone in the meadow. Getting up, Patricia walked toward the sound.

She came to the shack by the creek and thought, *It has been fixed up. It no longer looks like an old shack; it looks like a home!* Walking in, she was surprised to see curtains on the windows, a hand-carved table and chairs in one corner, and a beautiful bed made of cedar in another. *It looks so homey! Did John make all of this by hand?* She had been so surprised, she momentarily forgot her pursuit of the strange sound). Having left the door open when she entered, she again heard the sounds of splashing.

Quickly, silently, she exited the shack and walked toward the creek. There, swimming in the sparkling water, was John McDougal. The sight of him embarrassed

Patricia. She wanted to run away but was awestruck by the sight of him; never having seen a man before, as she was just fifteen. Again, something deep within her stirred. I mustn't be seen! She crouched behind the trees as John swam in her direction, his body glistening in the bright sunlight. She spied his clothes nearby. Picking up his handkerchief, with one last quick look, she ran all the way back to the estate.

Sometime later, one evening as she was alone in her room, she began thinking. *He doesn't know I exist. Why did I take this?* Tracing the embroidered initials with her fingers, she thought, *He's just an ordinary man.* But deep down inside, she knew differently. She knew the answer to her question. Tucking away the handkerchief in a secret spot, she dressed for bed.

Mother came in directly, as she did every night. Sitting together on the bed, Mother brushed Patricia's beautiful, long hair as they talked. Patricia always cherished this time alone with her mother. Hearing rustling outside, Patricia inquired. "Did you hear something outside?"

"No, dear, why?" The pair walked to the window but saw nothing when they looked outside. Patricia walked over to the window again when she was alone. She saw

15

nothing unusual, just the lamp in the hayloft and a form she assumed to be that of John McDougal. He had moved to the barn last week; Jasper (a distant relative working as a farmhand) had been living in the barn for two years now. She didn't know why John had been moved, but it made her happy to think of him so close. She ran her fingers across his handkerchief with this thought lingering. Smiling contentedly, she went to bed, dismissing the sounds outside completely.

John had become drawn to Patricia, and told Jasper his feelings. He had to know if she was just like all the others or if she was truly as different as she appeared. Almost every night, John rolled his blankets so that if anyone looked, they would assume he was there. Then he would stand beneath Patricia's window. His feelings for her had grown in such a short time. He marveled at the thought of her in her room in her nightclothes, speaking to her mother so innocently. Could she be as young as she appeared and hide her worldliness from her mother? Was she that good an actress? John had known many who were. No man would touch a girl who had been sullied. John was no different. When he did settle down, he wanted a virgin for a wife. After several weeks of listening, he came to

16

believe that Patricia was truly still innocent. She was not acting.

Maybe this is the time to talk to her, Patricia thought. As Mother finished brushing her hair, she placed her nightcap on her head. Playfully, Patricia took it off and tossed it aside. "I hate this nightcap, Mother!" Mother picked it up and again placed it on her daughter's head. As she did so, she buttoned Patricia's nightgown to her neck as she always did. As she bent down to kiss her on her forehead, Patricia began tugging at the buttons. "They're choking me! I'm afraid I'll never be a woman!" she blurted out loudly.

Mother looked at her for a minute, smiled a big, warm smile, and hugged her reassuringly. "Don't worry, dear. You'll be a woman soon enough." She sat down on the bed and undid the top button on Patricia's gown. "It will be our secret," Mother said as she rose to her feet.

In a wink, the mood turned from playful to serious. Mother sat down again at Patricia's side. "Patricia, you are becoming a woman. Your father has decided it is time for you to begin receiving gentleman callers immediately. He has set up some proper suitors for you. They will begin arriving the day after tomorrow. It is time for you to begin looking for a husband, my young one."

Mother's eyes were filled with tears, Patricia's with fear. "But Mother, what will I do?"

"You will receive each gentleman caller graciously and spend some time getting to know each of them. We will discuss this more tomorrow, Patricia."

Most of Klaus's business was conducted behind closed doors, so Patricia saw very little of her father. Each evening after supper, however, he enjoyed a glass of brandy and a smoke on the front porch swing. Ritually, he would settle himself down on the swing with his freshly poured brandy and savor it from the first drink until the glass was sufficiently empty.

This was a private evening ritual, but if one were to sneak a look, they would see him examining the glass, almost inspecting it, holding it up to the fading light and turning it between drinks. He seemed to become a different person when he was indulging himself each evening. The businesslike facade would slowly fade. What remained was a less stuffy but still reserved man, a man who wanted to let go but couldn't. Margaret had tired many months earlier of Klaus's "evening ritual," so she began watering down his brandy.

One night, he complained loudly of his brandy tasting weak and unacceptable. It was later discovered that some of the brandy had been poured out and replaced with molasses water.

Another evening, Father came out to the porch swing after having his brandy, to complete the ritual. After having trouble lighting his pipe, he settled back and inhaled deeply as always. Immediately he lunged forward, beginning to choke; Cook frantically rushed a cup of water to him. Mother ran outside fretting. No one had ever heard such sounds from Mr. Heifelmeyer. There was quite a flurry of activity around the house that night. When he had recovered his composure, Father dumped the pipe's contents out on the ground, hitting the bowl angrily against the swing, making sure it was empty. He bent forward to pick up the tobacco. As he brought it closer, he noticed the stench of horse manure! Jasper took the blame for that, even though it had been John who had switched the tobacco for manure.

Chapter 3

Suitors

Eighteen months later, Jasper and John had become quite good friends since sharing the same quarters. John confided in him his love for Patricia. When John asked for his help in building a home for the two of them, Jasper readily agreed.

And so the work was begun, secretly, on their own time. John had selected a small clearing that held the fresh morning light like a cup of tea, still and lucent. Whenever possible, John would sneak off for a bit to work on the house too, but only after his other work was completed. The fact that John left to work on the home was not openly known until much later.

Patricia also loved John very dearly. But neither confided their love to one another, so the few suitors Patricia had been receiving continued and increased upon Father's insistence. A girl of her breeding should be betrothed by now. Over the next months, suitable men were interviewed by Father, and times were arranged for meeting with Patricia.

It all seemed so businesslike. But then, much of what Father did seemed that way. Many teas were planned. Mother and Patricia entertained much more now than before. Mother was very subtle in her way. A ladylike hint dropped at the appropriate time was all that was needed. Mother was sure that the ladies of the community would let it be known that Patricia was accepting suitors.

The first two suitors Patricia entertained were high society, rich and stuffy, a third suitor, pompous. Secretly, she implored Mother's help: "I can't stand them!" Meeting times continued to be arranged, but the suitors never arrived. Again secretly, she met with Mother. "Thank you for putting an end to all of this."

"What do you mean, Patricia? I've had nothing to do with the suitors not showing up."

John had found out what was going on. He had been under Patricia's window the night Mother had informed her to expect suitors. He took time the very next day to enlist the help of Jasper and Cook to help stop all suitors making their way to see Patricia. Jasper and John spoke at length about "the Old Man," Patricia's father, as Jasper had been with the family much longer than John. Jasper was of the opinion that he was good for

Patricia. John was fuming at the thought of Patricia seeing others. Jasper was eager to help John whittle down the Old Man's list of prospective gentleman callers.

The decision was made then, to stop all suitors before they reached the house. John and Jasper always worked as a team and this would be the exception. One would remain working at all times in case the Old Man came along unexpectedly. With the help of Jasper (and Cook on occasion), John knew full well the exact times suitors were coming. He would ride out to greet prospective suitors, unbeknownst to anyone (except Jasper and Cook). He would explain, "You have been misinformed, Miss Patricia is spoken for! She is mine!" Upon hearing this, they would turn tail and run.

"Mother, I need to speak to about something very important."

"Yes, dear?"

"How will I know if I am in love with someone?"

Mother had anticipated this talk for a long time. "Well, dear," she began, "feelings are a very complicated thing. You must first carefully consider what you are feeling before you decide anything; do not jump to any conclusions. Young girls can easily confuse infatuation and love. Unfortunately, there are

23

girls who decide to act first and do not think about their actions; some even suffer consequences of their unwise decisions, having a child out of wedlock. It is always best to discuss this subject with your mother, dear. Be patient, Patricia, you will know when you are truly in love. You will feel the truth here" she said as she touched her own heart. "You will also know the gentleman's true feelings if you truly listen to him and he is honest with you."

"Have you met the new overseer Father hired?"

"Yes, I believe his name is John McDougal. Why?"

"Because I think I love him."

≈

"Jasper, get your hands off me, let me go! I'm going to tell the Old Man Patricia's in love with me. He needs to know, and I can't and won't put it off any longer!"

Jasper had to stop John more than once from barging in to the Old Man and making him aware of his intentions. "John, now is not the time, especially in the fury that you're in! You'll be turned away promptly. There has to be another way."

One suitor, however, did manage to get to the estate, but only because John was involved in work. Patricia and this gentleman caller, Randall Cunningham, sat on the porch swing. Randall was of good stock and well-fixed financially. He stuttered, however, every time he tried to speak. Patricia remained a lady at all times, even though she was embarrassed for Mr. Cunningham, The meeting ended no sooner than she secretly hoped it would. The poor man, upon leaving, fell off of his horse!

John came out from his hiding place around the corner as the suitor rode away. Though Patricia thought he had just arrived, he had been there, quietly seething for most of the visit. John had finished his work for the day shortly after Patricia and Randall had sat down. Upon hearing them, he decided just to stay there.

His anger apparent as he came out from hiding, he roared, "That is enough, Patricia. I love you. I have from the day I arrived here, from the moment I met you over two years ago. You are going to be my wife! But being that you are a lady of breeding and I am a gentleman, I will formally ask you to be my betrothed."

Patricia was ecstatic; she didn't need to give it a second thought. "Yes," she whispered. "Oh, John, --" But before she could continue, he kissed her. Afterward, they sat down on the porch and held each other close. John looked rather surprised to find out that she'd had feelings for him for so long and told her mother of these feelings. He knew quite well what a strict family Patricia's was.

Later that week just an hour before sunset, they could wait no longer. John and Patricia decided to tell Mother even though Father was away.

"Mother, John and I love one another. We want to get married right away." "Patricia, John, I am so pleased for you both!" she replied, hugging them both. "But, dear, your father must be consulted! There must be a suitable courtship."

"Consult Father if you wish, but it is John that I'm going to marry. You have known for ages how I have loved him!"

"Yes, dear. I have known. But I thought it best that your father did not. He knows nothing of this."

"Mrs. Heifelmeyer," John finally said. "May I speak freely?"

"Yes, John."

"I have loved your daughter, dear Patricia, since the day I arrived in your home. I did not speak immediately because she was young and innocent. But over time, I have watched her grow and with that time, my love for her too has grown. She is soon to be seventeen, and I am twenty. I have asked Patricia to marry me, and she has graciously accepted. She is my life, ma'am. I am proud and happy to profess my love for her to you and my dear Patricia now, and to Mr. Heifelmeyer upon his return."

Jacob would do errands for Mother. He and the head maid were Mother's confessors. He was Trish's "shadow" since her birth. Jacob used nicknames for the family. They were My Lady Margaret for Mother; for Father, the Old Man; and for Patricia, My Little Papoose. Both Jasper and Jacob gave John permission to see Patricia, even though he didn't have the Old Man's permission yet.

Chapter 4

Asking for Her Hand

On December 27, 1866, John could wait no longer. He walked with purpose up to the house when Mr. Heifelmeyer was having his nightly brandy and asked to speak to him. "Sir, I would like to speak to you man to man."

He made an appointment for 8:00 in the evening to see Mr. Heifelmeyer so that he could ask for Patricia's hand. He was very nervous, as any young man would be in similar circumstances. He was shown in and told to wait in the study, and the doors were closed behind him. He sat down in a chair, expecting Patricia's father to be there at 8:00, but he didn't enter the study until half past the hour.

When Mr. Heifelmeyer came into the room, he didn't acknowledge the fact that John was even there. Walking directly to his desk, he sat down and began going over his ledgers. It was another full ten minutes before he even acknowledged the fact that John was

29

there. He had to clear his throat, in order to be noticed.

"How are things going on the estate?" For twenty minutes, Patricia's father discussed the estate with John, telling him he was the best overseer he'd ever had. He said he hoped to keep him on for quite a long time. In the future, John might even be allowed to buy a plot of land from him to build a home on and work his own land in addition to staying on and working for Klaus.

Klaus was not about to make this easy for him. After twenty minutes of discussing the estate, Klaus said, "Well, if the estate is fine and you didn't come to speak about that, then why are you here?"

By this time, John was so nervous, he thought he would just leave. He thought to himself, *No, I'm not going to let you scare me off. I came in here to ask for Patricia's hand in marriage and that's what I'm going to do!* Clearing his throat again, he began, "I'm, uh, here because I love your daughter."

"Well, everyone loves my daughter."

"Yes, sir, I'm sure they do, but I love Patricia in a special way. I love her with all my heart and soul." On impulse, John stood. "I came here this evening with one thought in mind. I came to declare my love for your daughter openly to you and to ask you for her hand in marriage. Patricia and I love one another, and we will be together." John was so nervous, he was jumping for the ceiling on the inside, his heart in his throat, as Mr. Heifelmeyer moved abruptly in his chair exclaiming, "Indeed."

"You are a worldly man, John. Patricia is an innocent child. You haven't destroyed that, have you?" Klaus boomed and stood up with his hands on his hips. John felt as if the entire room shook with his fury.

"No, sir. No! I love Patricia. I adore her, sir. I want to marry Patricia and take care of her forever!" Standing his ground, he continued, "I would much rather have your permission, but either way, we will be together." *There, I've said it.* He hoped Mr. Heifelmeyer didn't notice how scared to death he really was.

Clearing his throat and adjusting his shirt collar, Mr. Heifelmeyer said, "Sit down, son; sit down," as he seated himself.

"No, thank you, sir."

"How do you plan to do this, assuming I give my permission?"

"I've already been working on a home for us, sir, on the north end of the property. I've worked on it for almost a year now."

"Yes, John. I am aware of the home."

"I will continue to work for you if you wish. If not, I will acquire other work. Patricia will not lack for anything, if I have my way. I would give her the moon if she asked for it."

Well over an hour after Mr. Heifelmeyer entered the study, they both emerged. Emotionally and physically drained, John left the house. He was sure that his hair was more silvery now than at the beginning of the conversation. Indeed, months later, a soft streak of white appeared just above his right temple.

Mr. Heifelmeyer refused to allow a wedding as soon as the couple wanted. However, with considerable prodding on the part of Mrs. Heifelmeyer, they agreed to a minimum of a three-month courtship.

Even so, that was close to a scandalous amount of time for a courtship. Usually in New Orleans, courtships lasted a maximum of eighteen months. It was agreed that they would be wed on her seventeenth birthday, April 6, 1867.

Chapter 5

The Wedding

The excitement was palpable as plans were made for the upcoming nuptials. Family and friends were invited, and Father's business associates too. Mother and daughter chittered happily like two squirrels over a newfound bounty of nuts as they sat together admiring the invitations, laboriously folding, sealing, and addressing them as they talked. The invitations were printed on bands of white ribbon and mounted on white parchment and delivered by hand through family servants.

Life was very happy since they had confided their love to one another. Still, they were not allowed to see each other after 8:00. Patricia spoke often, when they were together, of how much happier they were since they had told each other of their feelings. "Of course, silly!" John would say, reaching for her hand and laughing. Oh, how she loved that laugh and magical twinkle in his eyes! Time passed quickly.

On the eve of their wedding, Patricia was visited in her room, as always, by her mother; this time, Mother had brought with her a large box. "This is for you, dear."

Patricia took the box from her and opened it excitedly. As she pulled back the last of the wrappings, she gasped in wonder at what she saw. It was the most beautiful petticoat she had ever seen! Slowly, carefully, she pulled it out of the box.

"Oh, Mother, it's beautiful!" She stood up with it, ran to the mirror, and held it up in front of herself. Watching Patricia, Mother thought, *She looks so grown up, so beautiful with her long hair cascading down her back, and tomorrow she is to be wed.* Tears came.

"Oh, thank you, Mother. I love it!" she squealed, looking at in the mirror and running her fingers over the delicate lace and daisies on the petticoat. Her eyes shone with delight. The entire petticoat was layer upon layer of white lace with tiny, hand-embroidered daisies strewn throughout. Mother sat on the bed watching her twirl round and round in circles as she held the petticoat up in front of her. Her soul smiled at Patricia's happiness.

Patricia ran back to her mother and hugged her tightly. Mother laughed, pleased, and hugged her back. Smiling, she said,

"Now, sit down. It is time we had a talk." Patricia sat down, looking questioningly at her mother. "Tomorrow you will be wed."

"Yes, Mother."

"There are a few things that you and I must discuss. Being married is very joyous, for the most part. You have someone to share your special feelings with, a companion; someone with whom to share the good times and the bad times. You will be taken good care of, but you must do as you are told to. Your husband is the master of the household. His word is law. You must obey him. If you are lucky and try very hard to please him, you will have a very good life.

There are things too, daughter, that you must learn to endure. What I will tell you now is of great importance, so listen well; there is one part of marriage that is not so pleasant. In fact, at times it can be very painful, but you must, and you will learn to endure it. It is your 'wifely duty.'"

"Yes, Mother," she said with a look of concern and the tiniest bit of fright in her voice.

"When you marry, your husband acquires certain rights to you. Rights that he can demand that you give him, and you must submit to it. It is part of being a wife. It may be a hard thing to do at first, but you will

36

learn to put up with it. You must; it is your wifely duty."

Even though Mother explained fully, this concerned Patricia terribly. She did not see how John could ever be cruel to her or hurt her. She tried to forget her fright of this scary, secret thing that would happen to her, but no matter how she tried, the mere thought of it and the fright she felt concerning it loomed heavily in her thoughts. The next morning, Patricia rose early. She couldn't bear to wait any longer. She was so excited—today was her wedding day! She began by brushing her hair as she always did. She loved the feel of her hair, so soft, full, and thick. Soon, Mother came in to awaken her. Not surprised to see Patricia already up and about, she drew her bath.

Patricia knew that she had some extra time, and that was just what she wanted; time to relax and prepare for the important day ahead of her. She pulled her hair up on her head so she could bathe. She wanted to take extra special care of herself today. Today was special, and so was she. After bathing, she rubbed lilac all over her body. She loved its scent and was going to treat herself to it today.

As she began dressing, Mother came in again to help her. Patricia reached for the beautiful petticoat Mother had given her the night before, again struck by its beauty. Putting it on, she ran her fingers over it again, as she had done the night before. Carefully, she picked up the gown she would wear on this special day. It was the dress Mother had worn on her wedding day; it was made of white silk, with puffed sleeves, a high waistline, and a scoop neckline, and closed with many buttons down the back. There was a small, pleated train. As she put it on, with Mother's help, she let it fall carefully to the floor. While Mother buttoned it for her, she ran her fingers over the beautiful silk gown. It was a perfect fit. Slowly, she turned to Mother, her eyes filled with tears.

"Oh, Mother, it's so beautiful! Thank you for letting me wear it. It means so much!"

They embraced. As they separated, Patricia noticed tears in Mother's eyes too. As if they were of one mind, they both said, "I love you." Drying her own eyes and Patricia's, Margaret viewed Patricia as a woman for the first time. She took Patricia by the hands. "Be happy. John is a good man. He will be good to you. "Then Mother handed her the new lace handkerchief and scarf they had bought for her to wear and gave her the bonnet that completed her outfit. The bonnet was pleated on top of the crown, had white satin ribbon ties, and was just as beautiful as the gown.

Patricia sat down on her bed to put on her slippers. They were very delicate—white satin with leather soles and white ribbon ties. Before rising, she made final adjustments to her white silk stockings and white satin garters with their gleaming gold buckles. Patricia was a sight to behold. She reminded Margaret very much of herself on her wedding day so many years ago.

Patricia loved this gown. She could have had a new one—one all her own, one much fancier if she had wished it. She could have had any gown she wanted. It pleased her mother that she chose to wear her gown. Sentiment was much more important to Patricia than an expensive gown. True, her family was well off, but she did not like flaunting what she had. It wasn't important to her. In fact, most of the time, she was happiest when people didn't know about it. Then she could be treated as anyone would. Patricia thought it very shallow of some people to treat her and her family with greater respect and courtesy because they were well to do. She felt it should make no difference; what you had should not be nearly as important as what you are.

As they finished getting her ready, Mother handed Patricia a handkerchief. "It's the one I used at my wedding. I want you to have it. You look beautiful, dear."

Just then, Father knocked and entered the room. He was taken aback by the sight of his grown little girl. "Come here, Patricia. I want you to see something." Taking her outside, he walked her over to a wagon and team that she had never seen.

"Is there someone here, Father?"

"No, Patricia. They are for you and John from your mother and I." Awkwardly, he hugged her. Patricia stood there, gently in a state of shock. She mumbled, "Father?"

"Yes, Patricia. They are yours."

Turning and hugging him, she said quietly, "Thank you, Father." Finally, all was prepared, and they were off to the chapel. Father drove the new wagon, with two horses following behind. Patricia was lost in her thoughts. *The wagon is so beautiful! I can't believe it. Today is already so wonderful, and I haven't even seen John yet!* Looking around the wagon, feeling the wood, Patricia was in awe at the smoothness of the wood under her touch. *It's newly made; the lumber smells freshly cut. It's large, roomy enough that all of our supplies and belongings could be transported anywhere.* Patricia, still lost in thought, was unaware of the fact they had come to a halt. She startled when Mother tapped her.

"We're here, dear. Are you all right?" Father was at her side, ready to help her out.

"Yes, I'm fine."

As they entered the chapel, Mother made sure Patricia's train never touched the ground. Mother and daughter took time for final preparations as the last of the guests were seated.

John and Jasper were in their places up front, speaking with Reverend Williams. Jasper looked up as Mr. Heifelmeyer was coming forward to join the conversation. Realizing Patricia had arrived, and meeting her father halfway, Jasper excused himself to deliver the bouquet of wildflowers—daisies and lilacs John had picked for his bride.

"Thank you, Jasper, they are beautiful. How is John?"

Before Jasper had time to reply, Patricia saw John in conversation with Reverend Williams and her father. John looks extremely handsome in his suit. It consisted of pearl-gray breeches, shirt, waistcoat, and tie. The sight was breathtaking to Patricia. I've never seen John in anything but his work clothes. He looks so different; yes, I know well that he is a handsome man, but today, in this suit, he is even more handsome than I could ever have imagined!

The ceremony was a small one, just as the couple wanted. As they began, Patricia's father walked her down the aisle and presented her to John. As he saw her coming down the aisle, his eyes widened, his lips parted slightly, and he drew in a breath. Their eyes met, and the ever-present twinkle shone brightly. John took a step toward them. Extending his hands to Patricia, he gently clasped hers, whispering, "You look beautiful!" She blushed.

The ceremony began, with Patricia's eyes cast downward to conceal her nervousness. It was a formal ceremony as most couples planned with only their closest family members in attendance. Patricia appeared to John to be at a type of mental doorway, ready to step across the threshold to join him. John's attention too, was drawn away from the words Reverend Williams was reciting. Shortly, both came back to the present.

"May I say, it is apparent to all here present," they heard the Reverend addressing them, "what a special couple you are. Your love is not hidden under a bushel basket, but shining brightly today. I am privileged to be here with you as your servant before the Lord.

John, wilt thou have this woman for thy wedded wife, to live together after God's ordinance in the holy estate of matrimony? Wilt thou love her, comfort her, honor and keep her in sickness and health; and forsaking all others, keep thee only unto her, as long as ye both shall live?"

"I will."

"Patricia, wilt thou have this man for thy wedded husband, to live together after God's ordinance in the holy estate of matrimony? Wilt thou love him, comfort him, honor and keep him in sickness and health; and forsaking all others, keep thee only unto him, as long as ye both shall live?"

"I will."

With the rings placed on the bride's finger at the conclusion of the vows, Reverend Williams paused. John had asked him to do so at this point in the ceremony when he arrived earlier that morning.

John held Patricia's hands and kissed them tenderly as he began, "You are my heart, Patricia, and neither of us is whole alone. My dear Patricia, I want to keep the sparkle in your eyes burning brightly forever. The vows that I have just spoken will not be just until death. You have my heart and my love forever and always. I want you, and all here present to be witness to my eternal pledge to you."

Caught off guard, Patricia regained her composure quickly. Filled with even deeper emotion, squeezing his hand, she began, "I too wish to pledge myself eternally to you in the presence of this company, John. You are my life. I breathe for you and with you. I want to share every moment with you, not just now, but forever and always, 'til the end of time."

As the bride finished, Reverend Williams concluded the ceremony. "Let no man separate what God has joined."

≈

The wedding had been so long in coming, the couple felt. Not for reasons of lust, as Patricia's parents secretly feared, but simply because of their mutual need to be together always. They wanted to share everything, from the laughter and good times they had recently shared to every aspect of each other's daily existence.

Patricia's parents need not have feared for their daughter's virginity. It was still very much intact and treasured by her, and that is what Patricia considered it: a treasure and a gift to be given to her husband, to be opened

for the first time on their wedding night; and
so it would be.

Chapter 6

Celebration!

After the ceremony, everyone returned to the house for a reception. The house was gaily decorated with blue and white flowers strung across the porch banisters. It was the social event of the year, with quite a large number in attendance. The bride and groom mingled with guests until two debutantes stopped them and wanted to admire Patricia's wedding attire and her beautiful ring. John politely excused himself and joined his father-in-law who took the opportunity to introduce him to some important business associates. The reception proceeded without incident until one of Patricia's ex-suitors, Randall Cunningham, began to get rather inebriated and monopolize the bride's time. Patricia wished he would just go away so she could rejoin John and their guests, but she remained a lady. She had already danced with him once, and he kept stepping on her feet.

John had been talking with Jasper, and he had indeed seen what had been going on. "Do you want me to handle this for you, Trish?" (John's endearing name for Patricia was Trish and only he called her by that name).

"I can take care of myself, thank you."

I guess I'll just go back and talk to Jasper and watch how she takes care of things. She began another dance with Randall. Toward the end of the dance, he stepped on Patricia's wedding gown and the bottom of the train tore. Patricia picked up the torn section of her mother's gown and began to cry. Moments later, Randall ushered Patricia to the settee in the far corner of the room. When John looked over at them, Randall was talking to her very intently. It looked as if he were trying to comfort her. She looked at John with the word "help" in her eyes.

She can wait just one minute longer while I finish my conversation with Jasper. When he looked again, the look of "help" had been replaced with a look of fire. Leaving Jasper, John thought, *What a way to start a wedding night!* The closer he got, he saw tears in Trish's eyes and the torn wedding gown she held like an injured child. John filled with an anger he had never felt before.

"Randall, you have monopolized my bride's time long enough. I suggest you mingle a little."

"No, thank you."

"Then leave. You are no longer welcome here." By now, Patricia's parents had moved closer, not to interfere, but to better observe.

"But," Mr. Cunningham began in protest. John put his arm around the man's shoulder and talked to him in a low, calm voice while walking him outside.

Once out of sight of the guests, John bodily picked him up placed him on the banister of the front porch. In the state Randall was in, more than slightly inebriated, he couldn't keep his balance and fell off the porch.

Shortly after, the newlyweds prepared to leave. As they did, Jasper asked John if he could speak to Patricia. When they were alone, he began, "Well, did you enjoy taking care of yourself?" Before she could speak, he continued, "John is your husband now. He will not only love you and provide for you, he will protect you. You should have let him take care of the situation when he first asked.

Even if you can take care of something yourself, Patricia, let him feel that he is needed. That is very important to a man. Make him feel as special as he makes you feel. The love you share is a treasure and a gift from God. Remember this, and treasure him. Now, go to him, Little One, and be happy!"

With a demure thank you and a big hug for Jasper, she returned to John. The couple bid their good byes and were off, leaving behind her parents, who were still quietly chuckling over the incident on the porch earlier. Patricia turned back for a final good bye to her parents and noticed tears in their eyes.

As soon as they were out of earshot, Patricia couldn't be quiet any longer. She was sure that if she did, she would burst.

"John," she began breathlessly, "what shall we do? We have no place to live. No—" But before she could continue, John interrupted.

"Quiet, my love, and come with me," he replied, taking his new bride's hand. As he spoke, she saw a magical twinkle in his eyes. Patricia hushed and followed John's lead. He helped her into the new wagon and urged the horses to a trot. She sat close to him, her left hand on his thigh, her right in her lap, thinking, But where are we going? Patricia's curiosity was stronger than ever.

Chapter 7

New Beginnings

The ride seemed endless. Gradually they came to a halt in front of a cabin, one Patricia had never seen before. Saying nothing, John got out of the wagon and came around to help her. As he did, he was distinctly aware of her confusion. He led her slowly in front of the team until they came to a specific spot and stopped. She noticed that twinkle as he turned toward her.

"Welcome home, my love," he said quietly with a great sense of pride.

"John?"

"Yes, love, this is our home. I began building it over a year ago. Come and see." He swept her up in his arms. Once across the threshold, he set her down just inside the door. She looked around the room slowly. There was a table and chairs set up by a small but beautiful rock fireplace, which was complete with a huge iron pot and cooking utensils.

John carried her to their bedroom. The next morning during breakfast, they shared memories of the reception. Patricia remembered Randall's fall from his horse as he left.

John chuckled. "Well, I have to take part of the blame for that. You see, I was more than just a little upset at his monopolizing you. I was going to go over and give him a piece of my mind and throw him out, but Jasper calmed me down. Instead, I went outside and loosened up his saddle a bit." The thought of Randall falling off had them both laughing to the point of tears.

As days turned to months, they remained as close as they had been on the day they wed. John would leave the house in the morning to cut down trees at the property lines. In truth, there were no definite properties, since the home had been built on the extensive Heifelmeyer estate. Property lines did exist to some extent, but only for the sake of privacy.

In good weather, Trish would set about baking a pan of biscuits as soon as he left. As soon as they cooled a bit, she would wrap them in a towel for the journey across the acres to see John and offer him the freshly baked biscuits. It became a tradition with the couple; a special time to share themselves with each other.

≈

John had vowed he wouldn't keep anything from Trish. Early morning April 19, 1867, they sat together talking, when John pulled booklets from his back pocket.

"My love, I must tell you something. I have joined Pinkerton's National Detective Agency. I want you to read these booklets. They can explain better than I."

Trish took them and began reading. As she turned the last page, she reached for his hand and kissed it tenderly.

"John, I agree with everything here. I totally support your decision." John reported directly to Allen Pinkerton.

Chapter 8

Becoming a Family

She had been thinking of him, looking at the beautiful wedding ring he had given her. It would seem quite plain to some, but she cherished it. I cannot believe that we are truly married. I feel as if I have always loved him, and I am quite sure that I will never stop loving him. John fills my heart completely. I have everything I've ever truly wanted – a God-given gift of everlasting love and companionship, and a life-long friend.

Glancing again at her ring, she smiled as she watched the two ruby chips dancing in the sunlight. Patricia felt as warm as the sunshine, filled with love for John. She had come to know what to expect from his touch. When he traced her face with his fingers ever so lightly, he was warm, loving, and romantic. If he caressed her cheek, lingeringly cupping it in his hand, they would make love.

Seeing John come in, she smiled and walked over to him. He wore no shirt despite the slight chill in the air. After he stacked the armload of wood he'd been carrying, he turned to her and smiled. Reaching up to his shoulders, she slipped a finger under each of his suspenders and ran them down to his waistline. As she reached his waist, she welcomed him home with a kiss. He immediately responded to her as he always did.

Out of that love, their firstborn child was conceived that very night. Three months later, Trish was sure of her condition. She walked out to where he was chopping wood with a cup of cool water for him.

"John," she began as she handed him the water, "I have a surprise for you." She placed a hand on her stomach. "I'm going to have your child."

He had been drinking the water she'd given him as he listened. When he heard what she said, the cup dropped to the ground, and he stood looking at her, dazed. "John? Are you all right?" she asked as she touched his face.

Her touch brought him out of it. He picked her up and swung her around, both of them laughing and crying with joy. He set her down and kissed her. As they kissed, he realized what he had just done. Immediately, he went into a panic. "Oh, my gosh!" Scooping her up in his arms, he brought her back into the house, taking her over to the bed, and had a look of concern she had never seen before. "Are you all right, Trish?"

"Yes, silly! We're fine."

"A baby! Trish, I can hardly believe it! I'm so happy! You're sure you're all right? Should I fetch a doctor? Can I get you anything?"

She thought John's concern was very touching but hardly necessary. Smiling, she began to get up, but John stopped her.

"No. You stay here. I'll do whatever you need done." He was determined to pamper her, and pamper her he did. From the beginning, he was very protective of her. He refused to let her carry any water from the creek or lift anything heavy. If John had his way, Trish would have stayed in bed the entire pregnancy. On certain things, Trish stood her ground. She was almost as determined as John. She kept telling him, "I don't want to be put on a shelf for the rest of my pregnancy!"

She didn't feel pregnancy was a sickness (as most people treated it). She felt more alive now than ever before. She tried explaining it to John. "Sweetheart," she began, "you put a new life inside me; you didn't make me sick. I feel wonderful; I'm happier now than I've ever been before. Please don't worry so much; I won't break, and you won't hurt me. Let me do some things, honey. I need to. You don't want to spoil me, now do you? If you keep this up, I may forget how to do things. You wouldn't want that, would you?"

"No, Trish, I'm just so worried about you. I want you to be comfortable and happy."

"I am comfortable. Now make me happy." Some compromises were made. John now helped Trish with much of the work, especially cooking and laundry. He refused to let her lift heavy baskets of wet clothes or the iron pot at the fireplace. Secretly, Trish loved all of the pampering. She remembered what Jasper had told her the day she married John. She loved the way he looked at her now, with such concern and love in his eyes.

As time marched forward, they fell deeper and deeper in love. Her belly began to swell with child. Months later, upon retiring, Trish felt something move in her belly. "What's that?"

"What?"

"That!" she exclaimed, feeling it again and jumping. Together, they looked at her belly. The baby was moving, kicking; they watched together in total amazement.

"I can feel that!" she cried, reaching for his hand. She placed it on her belly just as the baby kicked again. John pulled his hand back as if she had put it on a bed of red hot coals.

Surprised at the movement, they both let out a laugh. John gently replaced his hand. She tenderly placed hers atop it. Smiling and contented, they fell asleep in each other's arms.

Late one evening, they sat talking on the floor in front of the fireplace as they often did, Trish leaning back, John with his arms around her.

"I still wonder sometimes where the daisies came from that were on my windowsill shortly after you arrived on the estate. I wore one of them in my hair for the longest time, remember?"

"Yes, and you looked so beautiful, even after it wilted!" John said with a grin.

"One of these days, I'll find out where those daisies came from!"

"You know, come to think of it, I lost a handkerchief while I was swimming one day. I never did find it."

Patricia looked like the cat that swallowed the canary. "I have a confession to make," she began, laughing quietly as she got up and walked to their dresser. She reached all the way to the back of the drawer, reaching for something. Walking back over to him and sitting down, she asked, "Is this anything like the one you lost?" Taking the object from her, he examined it. It was his handkerchief. It had his initials hand-embroidered in the corner.

"You?"

"Yes, me. I stumbled across you that day and took it. I didn't know why then, but I took it anyway."

"You were at the creek that day?"

"Yes," she replied, blushing.

Oh, how John loved it when she blushed! It made him melt.

"I've got a confession to make too. You know those daisies you keep wondering about?"

"Yes."

"Well, I threw them inside your window from below and stayed down there too. When your mother came in later, and you were talking with her, I heard every word. Do you remember what you said about being afraid you'd never become a woman?"

"Yes, I remember," she said quietly, blushing again. "The noise you heard outside was me."

"You?"

"Yes, and you almost caught me, too! If you had stayed at the window any longer, you probably would have spotted me."

"But I saw you in the hayloft!"

61

"You saw my blanket rolled up to look like me. I was under your window, hiding behind the tree."

"Oh, you!" she exclaimed, ruffling his hair and running. He caught her just as she ran past the bed. They fell back on the bed together, laughing and kissing.

≈

The closer the end of the pregnancy came, the more nervous John became. He knew the risks of bearing a child. He was thankful Trish did not. The next morning, Trish awoke to erratic pains. John went to fetch Doc. When he returned, he had not only brought Doc but Jasper too. Margaret also came by to check on Trish, as she knew her time was near. He let mother and daughter have time alone. In a short time John rushed back into the house to check on Trish, with Jasper close on his heels, only to be turned away by Doc.

By now, the birth process was beginning. Jasper and John sat down on the porch to wait. John was sure when the time came he would be calm; he turned out to be very wrong. He was more nervous now than he had ever been in his entire life. Suddenly, they heard a cry of pain from Trish. It was all Jasper could do to keep John outside.

The next cry they heard wasn't Trish, but that of their child. When John heard it, there was no holding him back, not that Jasper would have tried. John rushed in to her side. On seeing his firstborn wrapped in a blanket in Trish's arms, there were tears of relief and joy.

"Come see your son, love," Trish said as she motioned him closer. John was overwhelmed with emotion. Doc, Margaret, and Jasper stayed well back, not wanting to intrude on the couple's happiness. John leaned over to kiss his wife. She smiled and held out his firstborn to him. Gingerly, he took the baby from her. Trish smiled even brighter at the sight of them together. John filled with an overwhelming sense of happiness and pride when he laid eyes upon his firstborn son.

"Congratulations, you two!" Jasper told them, finally coming forward, smiling at Trish, winking at John.

"Thank you, Jasper".

Soon, John returned the baby to Trish and he kissed her again, whispering, "I love you, darling, more than I can say." After making sure that Trish and the baby were all right, he went over to talk to the doctor and

Jasper. Margaret came forward to see her first grandchild. She remained by Patricia's side while John spoke to the doctor and Jasper.

After seeing them all on their way, he came back in to his family. He was awestruck by the sight of Trish putting her babe to breast. The baby was hungrily suckling, his tiny hands kneading.

The sight filled him with such unbelievable joy. It wasn't only Patricia's body he loved; he loved her mind, her sense of humor, and her passion for life. In fact, these qualities first attracted him to her.

She could make his heart skip a beat just by looking at him. The laughter they shared was priceless. Their life together was invaluable beyond comparison to him, as it was to her.

They didn't have much to call their own, monetarily speaking, but what they lacked in these areas was made up for in the wealth of love and friendship they shared together.

They both reveled in the new life God given to them, Johnny. Every day was a new experience. The new parents could never have imagined how much more fulfilled life would be with a child; the faces they made together; watching their son discover his fingers, toes;

his tongue and his voice. Each new discovery the baby made was cause for celebration.

Trish felt such a new zest for life; she was so happy, she found herself constantly singing. And John! Well, he was the picture of a button busting new father. Constantly, you could spy him talking to his son, many times down on his hands and knees so that he could be eye to eye with Johnny. Every day, when John came in from his work outside, he would greet Trish, walk over to Johnny, pick him up, and twirl him gently 'round.

The baby's mastery of crawling, talking, and walking was met with great happiness and pride by his parents. As time marched on, so did Johnny—literally. Soon he was following Daddy out the door—first toddling after John, then walking, and soon after, running. Father and son spent an increasingly large amount of time together. They became inseparable. Trish became accustomed to the fact that where one was, the other was either there already or soon to follow.

For the first year, they made Johnny's bed in their room at night. Trish felt more comfortable knowing where he was and that he was all right. He was still much too young to realize what was going on between his parents.

Chapter 9

Two?

The couple kissed, hugged, and held hands quite often. It was not meant as a flagrant show of their feelings; it had become a natural part of their lives, as natural as breathing, to touch one another, each showing their love for the other in simple ways. They always kissed each other upon leaving or returning to the other's company.

The fire of their love was always glowing; the embers ready to re-ignite the passions they felt with a glance, a touch, or a spoken word.

"Trish, let's never hide what we have behind closed doors or 'under a bushel basket'. When we have children, I want them to be aware of our love for each other and to know how much they will be loved. You feel the same way, don't you?"

"Yes, John. I want to teach them they should never be afraid or ashamed to show their love for anyone or anything."

When Johnny was eighteen months old, Trish had another surprise for John.

Again, she was going to have his child. The family was growing, and she and John were ecstatic.

On their son's second birthday, Trish was six months along with their second child. There was quite a difference in the two pregnancies, though. This time she was much larger than before, which made things increasingly more difficult for her, the further along she was. The more Trish thought about it, she realized she had been bigger from the beginning this second time. Neither she nor John knew what to think of her increased size, and Doc said everything was fine.

They had a small birthday party for Johnny. He was having a wonderful time, being the center of attention, even more so than usual. When Daddy brought out his gift, he let out with a squeal of delight; it was a rabbit all his very own.

Trish sat down for a while to enjoy the sight of her husband and son together. It was a perfect day, filled with warm sunshine, sweet breezes, and happy voices. Just watching the two of them with that rabbit made her heart sing with happiness; both of their faces shone like the sun! Their joy and laughter was contagious. Johnny's eyes sparkled brighter than she'd ever seen them.

They were tiny, sparkling pools of blue. And, oh, how she loved to hear them laugh!

As the final weeks of Trish's pregnancy approached, both she and John became more apprehensive about the impending birth. They had both spent time talking to Johnny about the new brother or sister he would have, trying to prepare him. He began to change, seeming to understand that he would soon have to share Mommy and Daddy.

When her time came, Doc was fetched, and once again, John was summarily tossed out of the house. He had Jasper to keep him company in the long hours of waiting. This time they had the added attraction—or distraction—of Johnny.

John had become extremely concerned about Trish. Things were taking so much longer this time; John began thinking disastrous thoughts, and he allowed them to envelop him. All that was real melted away. He began to feel as if he were drowning, gasping for air, frantic for the sweetness of its smell.

Everyone waiting felt the tension. Jasper too was concerned about the time, but he didn't speak of it, for John's sake. Johnny became restless. Soon he lost interest in playing in the yard and remembered that Mommy was inside the house.

"Daddy, I want to go inside the house and see Mommy!" "No, Johnny! You stay out here." John boomed.

The boy shrank away from his father, frightened. Immediately, John realized what he had done. He got up from the porch where he had been sitting with Jasper, ran over to his son, and scooped him up in his arms, hugging him.

"I'm sorry, Johnny. I shouldn't have yelled at you. I know you want to see Mommy, honey; so do I. But we can't right now. Mommy is very busy. She's with the doctor, remember?"

"Is Mommy safe?" Before John could answer him, they heard a scream from inside the house. John jumped in surprise, tightening his grip on Johnny, who was still in his arms, and turned toward the cabin door.

"Mommy!" the child screamed.

Trying not to show his own fright to his son, John comforted him, saying, "Don't you worry, honey. Mommy is fine. The doctor is helping Mommy." In the same moment, he glanced to Jasper for support.

Father and son went back to the porch to wait. The two sat down side by side. As they did, Jasper, smiling through his concern, spoke reassuringly to the boy. "Of course your mommy will be all right, John. Your Mommy is pretty tough!"

They expected the doctor to come out soon and tell them that they could go in and see Trish and the baby. That was not the case, however; the time continued to drag on and on. What was really only minutes seemed like years. Later, they heard a second scream. Everyone outside stopped in their tracks. It was all John could do, not to go running in to Trish, but he knew if he did, Johnny would follow right behind him, so they waited and waited, the three of them together on the porch.

Finally, Doc did come out looking exhausted as he wiped the perspiration from his brow with a yellowed, ragged handkerchief. He looked up, sporting a broad grin, and announced, "Well, John, you have healthy twin girls! Trish is very weak but doing fine. You can go in, but only for a few minutes."

Jasper and John exchanged shocked expressions. Jasper caught up Johnny and hugged him tightly, dancing around the yard with the boy in his arms. Still numb with shock over Doc's announcement, John went into the cabin; he was in a daze, walking on air. Slowly he walked to their bedroom and

71

saw Trish lying quietly, her eyes closed, her face perspiration-soaked. Cradled in her arms were two little bundles. Quietly he approached the bed and whispered her name. She opened her eyes sleepily and smiled weakly.

"Hi, sweetheart."

Instantly, John was aware of how the birth had indeed weakened her; her voice was very strained. The uneasiness John had felt so strongly earlier returned. She spoke again, trying not to let John see how tired she was. Her voice is stronger but it's not as strong as it should be.

"Come here, Daddy, and meet your beautiful daughters." Unsure of her health, he came closer. "Are you all right, my love?"

Trish grinned from ear to ear. "Exhausted, but I think I'll make it. I

guess I'll have to; someone has to take care of this growing family."

John was astonished as he gazed at his daughters. "Honey, I can't believe this, two babies, and both girls."

Chapter 10

Introductions All 'Round

As John sat down on the bed, he was in awe. She motioned for him to take one of t hem. Picking up one of the sweet, war m, sleeping little girls, he felt the wonder of it all overwhelm him.

Minutes later, Johnny couldn't wait any longer. "I want to see my mommy!" he cried and took off running toward the cabin. Jasper and Doc caught up with him just as he got inside the house. Hoisting him up into his arms, Jasper looked to Doc for approval to continue.

With a nod and a smile, Doc said, "A quick visit, son. Mommy's very tired."

Silently, the two men entered the bedroom with the boy, motioning him to silence. On seeing them enter, John acknowledged them to come closer. Jasper set Johnny down next to his parents as the boy's eyes widened.

Proudly, John showed his son one of his sisters. The child reached out to touch the baby in his daddy's arms, filled with curiosity when her fingers moved at the touch. As he came to see his mommy, a look of genuine surprise and confusion came to his small, round face. He drew in a breath when he saw her holding another baby.

"Two babies?" His confusion grew by leaps and bounds.

Reaching out for him, she answered, "Yes, honey. You have two baby sisters. Would you like to see this one?" Trish took his hand and let him climb up on the bed next to her.

"They're so tiny," he kept repeating, looking from one to the other and back again.

Shortly, John laid his daughter down by Trish and took Johnny from the room, with Jasper following them out. After checking on mother and daughters, Doc joined the men outside.

Johnny was again playing in the yard. Jasper and John were talking together by the porch. When Doc joined them, John voiced his concern over Trish's weakened condition.

"Giving birth to twins was more difficult, John. With rest, though, she should recover in time. She did very well."

With further reassurances from Doc, John's concern lessened. Shortly, Jasper and Doc took their leave. Coming in to check on Trish and the babies, he found all three of them fast asleep. Jasper left for Kentucky shortly after the twins' birth.

Trish spent the next three days confined to bed, by John's orders. Although she pretended to be angry, she was quite satisfied to do so. The birth had drained her much more than she had expected it to, and she secretly loved being taken care of by "her men." Whenever Johnny came in to "take care of things," her heart burst with pride and delight.

For nearly two weeks following the birth, Trish was pampered by her men. John took care of everything, even straightening the cabin and preparing all of the meals. They both helped with the girls. Johnny had taken to his duties as big brother and was quite serious indeed. He even tried his best helping Daddy with the laundry. Watching the two of them try to wrestle wet laundry was a sight to behold—John, lifting the sheets out of the basket, with Johnny's assistance. As the sheets were lifted to the clothesline, Johnny would raise his arms as high as they would go and then jump to get them up there. Once, while the girls were sleeping, Trish watched the merry parade of laundrymen with feelings of pride and thankfulness that she had been so blessed to have such a caring, loving husband and son. She began to smile as she watched, then chuckle. By the time the second sheet was on the line, both of the laundrymen were soaked to the skin. Trish was almost on the floor with laughter.

John wanted to buy Trish something very special. Checking his funds, his heart sank. *I want to buy her a newborn lamb, but can't afford the high price they are being sold for. I'll do the next best thing. I'll get her a kitten.*

He came home, apologies on his lips. "Oh, John, she is darling! Please don't be upset, I love her. In fact, I am going to name her Baa."

Time seemed to crawl one minute and race the next for Trish. Her days were taken up now, it seemed, in a never-ending cycle of feedings. Not that she was complaining, really. The girls were healthy, hungry, and happy; her family was complete. The only real problem arose one cool spring evening.

Chapter 11

Cool Breezes Turn to Terror

Trish had the window in the cabin cracked open a bit so she could enjoy the cool breeze that had come up. She sat back in the rocker to indulge Mary, who lay in her mother's lap, hungrily sucking her fists. *How good it feels to settle back and relax.* As Mary began suckling, Trish brushed back her long, golden hair and inhaled deeply, smiling as the fresh, life-filled breezes embraced her.

I'm finally regaining my strength. From the far corner of the cabin, in the bedroom, she heard a noise. Trish looked around the cabin, thinking Johnny had come inside without her seeing him. She saw nothing; again, she heard the noise, a rustling sound, and it was growing louder. Suddenly, Elizabeth let out a loud scream.

Frightened, Patricia gathered up Mary and ran frantically in to see the cradle. Nervously lighting the lamp, she threw back the blankets covering Elizabeth. She lay there blinking her tiny, tear-filled eyes, flailing her chubby arms wildly, crying angrily. Trish

79

examined her and found nothing wrong. As she felt around by Elizabeth's feet, she ran her hand over a small hard lump in the blankets.

John ran inside after hearing Elizabeth's screams all the way out in the yard where he was stacking cedar. "Trish, what's wrong? Are you and the girls all right?"

"There's something wrong with Elizabeth!"

As he picked her up, something jumped out of the cradle. Examining her he reassured Trish. "She's fine, just startled, and hungry." As he comforted his daughter, a small furry head appeared from under the blanket. Looking down, he saw the kitten. "Look, Trish."

Rubbing against John's leg, purring loudly was Baa. "Oh, no! You mean?"

"Yes!"

"Baa, what are you doing in here?"

Relieved, they both sat down on the bed together. As if in silent communication, both girls let out a hungry wail. John occupied one daughter while Trish fed the other. Later, John tucked in Elizabeth, while Trish took Mary and put her babe to breast. When both were content Trish let out a contented sigh. God has blessed us so richly.

≈

Even now, almost three full months after the birth, John was adamant about Trish taking things easy.

"I feel much better, sweetheart. I need to get back to normal. You don't want me to get too used to all of this pampering, do you?"

"Yes. You should be pampered! You just birthed twins, Trish. I don't want you trying to recover too fast. I love you and I want to keep you. I worry about you."

"I'll be fine, dear," she replied, kissing him. Leaning into him, she wrapped her arms around him; he replied, embracing her and kissing her strongly.

"Don't worry, my love, I'm not about to do too much. I know that you worry—you make me feel special. I'm afraid you're stuck with me; I'm not about to leave you—now or ever!"

Upon Trish's insistence, John returned to work two days later. Early in the morning, he kissed Trish and the children good-bye and returned to the forest to work, axe in hand. The sun shone brightly that morning. He walked for a while, noticing the smells of the forest and letting the warmth of the sun engulf him; he began to whistle.

Trish was happy too, happy that all was well with the children and her recuperation was going so well. She felt almost fully recovered from the birth, even though it had been a hard one. She smiled as she thought of the surprise they all felt after Mary had been born, finding there was yet another to be born, Elizabeth. They knew that Trish was much larger with this pregnancy than the last one, but no one even remotely suspected that she had been carrying twins, not even Doc. Every time Trish looked at the girls, she felt they were a special gift from God. Of course, she felt that way about all her children. But there was still something special about the twins, something just below the surface that she had yet to figure out.

John had built a fire in the fireplace before he left. She was warming breakfast for Johnny and preparing to put her babes to breast. She turned away from the fire for a moment to change the girls, with Johnny following close behind to "help out."

Before she could turn around again, she smelled something, but couldn't tell just what it was. Johnny began pulling on her skirts. He wants to do a trick for me.

"Yes, Johnny, just a minute." He just kept on pulling; losing patience, she turned. "Johnny, what in the world is going on! I said to wait a minute!" Trish picked up the girls and turned to look at him and saw the terror in his face. Past him, she saw the table and chairs aflame! The red-and-white curtains she had sewn by hand were being consumed. A rush of sheer panic ran through Trish's being. Instantly, she felt a cold chill. For what seemed like forever, she stood there in a trancelike state, her feet nailed to the floor. All the while, Johnny stood next to her, hands clutched at his face, petrified, tears streaming down his cheeks, a look of unspeakable terror in his eyes.

Looking down at her son, she saw the last of Mary's blanket being consumed. She had laid it across her chair when she'd gotten up. In the coolness of the morning, she had decided to bring the chair closer to the fireplace when she fed the girls. The girls had woken up shivering. She had pulled the chair over to sit on top of the rug, directly in front of the fireplace earlier, and now the rug and blanket were gone; the last of the chair was on fire. *Oh God, no! This can't be happening!* her mind screamed in fear.

Finally, Trish pulled herself back to reality. Filled with terror, her mind raced with thoughts of John away in the forest, the children, and the responsibility of getting them all to safety. She shook Johnny to bring him out of his panic. "Johnny, honey, you're fine. We're all fine, but we must get out of here. Now, you look at Mommy and listen."

It was finally registering; he was sniffling now, looking at her with more tears ready to spill out of those beautiful, brown eyes. "Johnny, do you hear me?"

"Yes, Mommy, but I'm scared." He began to wail, fear overwhelming him.

"I am too, honey, but we must get out of here; it's up to us. Can we do that?"

"Yes, Mommy."

"All right, then, it's very important that you do exactly as Mommy tells you. I want you to hold on to Mommy's skirt and walk very close to me. We'll walk out of here together."

By now, the entire eating area of the cabin was engulfed in flames, which were quickly making their way to the door. If they didn't get out soon, there would be no chance of escape. Sparks flew everywhere; the heat was intense, the smoke blinding.

"We can do it, Johnny," Trish said reassuringly, hoping that he didn't hear the terror in her voice. Holding the twins tightly, covering their faces with a blanket from the bed, the four of them began their walk of terror through the fiery cabin to the safety awaiting them outside. Johnny didn't have to be told to hold on to his mother's skirt; he wasn't about to let go. Slowly, carefully they walked the thin path to safety.

When they were all outside, they dashed away from the burning cabin, away from the searing heat. When they were a safe distance away, Trish felt her knees giving way. She knelt on the ground with the twins in her arms and her son at her side. Uncovering the girls, she leaned over to Johnny and kissed him, reassuring him and telling him how proud she was of him.

"We're fine now, honey. Daddy will be here soon." Trying to keep it together, but shaking, Trish continued to comforted her children.

Not long after he got to the forest, John looked up, back toward the cabin as he always did when he was away from his family. He was thinking of his family and how happy they were, but this time when he looked up, he was frightened by what he saw—smoke.

He dropped his axe and began running like the wind back toward the cabin, faster and faster. The closer he got to the burning cabin, the more he could hear the crackling of the flames and feel the fierce heat.

Out of the forest he came from behind Trish, running at a mad pace. He saw only

Trish and Johnny. Racing on toward the inferno, his only thought was saving his baby girls. Trish screamed to him when she saw him, "John, we're all here!"

Turning to face her, he saw the girls in her arms. They were hidden from view by her form. Letting out a cry of relief and thankfulness to God, he ran to them.

Together they stood, watching their home burn to the ground. With Trish holding the girls, and Johnny in his father's arms, they stood praying to the Lord, thanking Him for their safety.

All was as well as it could be; the family was together and unharmed. All they had, other than the book of poetry, with its edges singed, was the clothes on their backs and each other; no matter, they were just thankful to be alive.

When the fire was out, all that was left of the cabin was the rock fireplace. Trish couldn't answer John when he asked how she had gotten herself and the children out of the fire. She couldn't remember, no matter how hard she tried. All she knew was that they had gotten out.

Thankfully, the barn had been far enough away from the flames that it hadn't been harmed. The family took up residence there. "When my body is no more, my soul will still be yours," John whispered, hugging his wife. "All I could think of was getting to you." he said shaking visibly. They sat together in the hay for a long while, holding each other, each comforting the other.

It would be a long time before Trish would recall how she and the children had gotten out of the fire. For months afterward, she relived the fire in horrible nightmares, waking drenched with sweat, shaking, screaming, crying hysterically.

In her dreams, she kept seeing the girls' blanket on fire. She would see herself trying to put it out and being unable to—unable to save her babies. The terror and helplessness she'd experienced during fire and couldn't let show for Johnny's sake was embedded in her soul. She saw the cabin engulfed in flames. She saw too, all that was left after the fire—the rock fireplace, charred and black from the heat of the fire, an everlasting reminder that it really happened. She saw herself, standing among the ruins, weary and alone. In her nightmares, things turned out quite differently than they had in reality; she was totally alone, her entire family taken from her.

John was also held helpless by her nightmares; he knew they must be about the fire, but she refused to talk about them, not now. He comforted her the best he could, holding her and stroking her hair.

Chapter 12

Rebuilding

Word of the fire spread quickly and within two days friends, neighbors and others that didn't even have a connection to the family from many Parishes turned out to help them rebuild, all carrying with them necessities for the family and children along with a bounty of foodstuffs for everyone.

"God's arms protected us from harm yesterday and now look at all of this!" John said as people and provisions just kept coming.

"Praise the Lord!" Patricia exclaimed at the sight. "John, how will we ever be able to return this much generosity? God is truly smiling on us today!"

A large piece of canvas was staked in the yard so the women could have shade while they prepared food for everyone and there were so many children!

Day after day they came cheerfully to help out, each day renewing the foodstuffs. Children's laughter was heard in the yard again.

"Lord, we are humbled to our core by Your grace. We are so thankful Father."

Groups of the men cut down trees while others rolled them a safe distance away to shape them into the size and number needed to rebuild. The new home was completed a week after the work began. It stood not far from the original one, within sight of the old fireplace. The new home was much bigger than the first. John and Patricia would finally be able to have a room all to themselves.

Thursday evening, after bedding the children, they sat close and spoke quietly and intimately. Even with all of the friends and neighbors also putting in hard labor and long hours, they too were both physically and mentally exhausted from their own hard work on the house raising.

Friday morning, Klaus watched his daughter as she bent over to pick up rocks to help complete the new rock fireplace. He couldn't believe the love that he witnessed between John and Patricia and the love and caring they both showed for their children. Witnessing John and Patricia together made him wish that he could feel and do for Margaret as John did for Patricia, but it was not in him to do so. He carried that ache was constantly in his heart.

John ran to Patricia's aid when she lifted a rock that was too heavy and strained her back. Klaus stopped before he reached her because he knew it wasn't his place anymore; it was John's.

John picked her up, brought her over to a tree and set her down to care for her. Johnny ran over to them, crying because his mommy was hurt. After comforting him, Patricia let Klaus and Margaret interest him in something else.

Soon, the painstaking work of completing the fireplace was finished, completed exactly the way Patricia wanted it, with the hearth extended outward an extra foot. She was positive that a spark from the old fireplace caused the blaze. She adamant that the new fireplace be made bigger.

There had also been a crew working on temporary furniture for the home. When the work was finished, late afternoon of the day Trish hurt her back, John took her into their new home and put her down on their new bed. He brought the twins in to lie near her. Johnny sat down on the bed and watched attentively as Daddy attended to Mommy.

As suppertime drew near, John finished making Trish comfortable and began to get supper for the family. Slowly, gingerly

Trish fed the girls, one at a time. Johnny was a big help keeping them busy for Mommy.

With supper over, John began bedding down the children for the night. As he tucked his son snugly into his bed and kissed him goodnight, he became aware that something was troubling the small child. There was a look of concern on his tiny face that outnumbered his years. Looking up with tear-filled eyes said, "Is Mommy okay?"

"Yes. Mommy will be fine. We just have to take extra-special good care of her for a while. Will you help me do that?"

"Yes, Daddy! I'll help! Can we pick some flowers for Mommy?"

"I think she would really like some flowers from her big boy! We'll do that."

"Night, Daddy."

"Good night, son."

John returned to check on Trish. The girls had finished suckling and all three were fast asleep. They all looked so contented, so happy! Taking each of the girls and bedding them down, he came back to his wife.

Smiling, he gently brushed her hair out of her face. She woke at his touch and reached up for him motioning him to sit down beside her; she grimaced in pain. Rising immediately, he tried to ease her discomfort.

Again, he tried to sit beside her and rose in response to her pain.

"I'll sit down on the floor next to you." Holding hands, they remained together for a long while.

As early evening turned to night, he helped Trish dress for bed, and the couple retired. Try as they might to lie together, they could not.

"No, I'll bed down here tonight." They fell asleep, side by side, Trish on the bed, John on the floor right below her, holding hands. John rested uncomfortably, but no matter. He kept hold of Trish's hand throughout the night, fearing that if he let go, she might awaken and feel the pain.

After four days and nights like this, Trish couldn't stand it any longer. "John, I hate sleeping without you here. Being hurt doesn't change how much I want to be with you either. I love you, and I want you with me here, in our bed. Yes, I hurt, but I still want you with me."

John smiled in response to his wife's demand that he bed with her. Reluctantly yet eagerly, he conceded to her demand. John was proud of Trish's strength and courage. He had never known another like her.

Gingerly he lay down by her, being sure to keep to his side of the bed so he would not hurt her. All the while, she held her breath as he got into bed. It had been four days since they lie together. She managed the physical pain of him getting into bed with some trouble, but she wasn't about to let him know that. As he settled in, she looked over at him across the sea between them. "John," she whispered softly, "Come here." He moved cautiously toward

his wife and engulfed her in his big protective arms. His embrace comforted Trish. It felt like home. They never slept apart again from that day forward.

Right after the fire, Klaus and Margaret discussed buying new furniture for John and Patricia. Costs were high, and making solid oak furniture again seemed out of the question due to the time it would take, but Patricia deserved the best. They invited the family over to the mansion for a meal. After dinner, Klaus told them he intended to buy all new furniture for the new home.

John became uncharacteristically angry and exploded. "No! Absolutely not! Are you implying I cannot provide for Patricia and the children? Well, I certainly can, and I don't need charity!" His every hair bristled.

"May I have a moment with my husband, please?" As her parents withdrew from the library, Trish began. "Why are you showing such disrespect to my parents; jumping down Father's throat when all he's ever done was to back you up? He has always stood with you, not against you, John."

As Trish spoke, John's anger melted away like snow on a warm day. "You are acting as if he is an enemy. All they want to do is help. Would you at least consider the offer?"

"I'm sorry, Trish. I feel very small right now. What I said was foolish; of course I will consider it."

John opened the library doors and invited his in-laws to come in. As they seated themselves, he began, "Sir, ma'am, I would like to apologize for my reprehensible behavior. There is no excuse." he said as he joined Trish on the couch, his eyes looking at the floor.

"Mother, Father, John is a wonderful provider for our family. I stand with my husband on this. He has provided well for me for many years, even prior to our marriage. We have spoken about your kind offer and wish to accept it if you still choose to offer your assistance. We would put only one condition on the acceptance, however. We are different people than you. I don't mean to imply that in a bad way; please let me

96

explain. We do not require the same elegance in furniture as you have; we only need furniture of the same quality that we lost in the fire. Is that acceptable to you?"

"It will be done as you wish, John, Patricia." "Thank you."

Chapter 13

Friends and Family

Five years after the twins, in 1877, there came another addition to the growing family, a plump, healthy girl. They named her Rebecca Anne McDougal. Becky was a happy child, always smiling and full of laughter. She was the mischievous one of the group. Her middle name should be "Curious," Patricia said constantly.

In the autumn of 1879, when Becky was two, John and Trish invited their close friends, Ethan, Lynn, and Ricky Kilkesen and Patricia's parents to the cabin for a picnic. Everyone brought food to share. The men played horseshoes, while the women prepared the meal. All the children played in the yard, making a plentiful amount of cheerful noise.

A picnic table and benches had been set up in the yard, close to the cabin. Light fall breezes were blowing, and the sun shone brightly on a glorious day. Patricia turned away from the preparations just in time to see Becky stick her pudgy little hand in a bowl of fresh orange marmalade. Becky looked with pride at her mommy and said, "See Mommy?" Seeing her daughter's bright smiling eyes, Trish came round the table to wipe the jellylike preserve from Becky's chubby little fingers.

Mary and Elizabeth helped Becky down and took her back in the yard to play with the others. Ethan, Klaus and John had a lively game of horseshoes going, with much laughter and banter between them. Johnny and Ricky (Ethan and Lynn's son) were in another part of the yard playing stickball. Lynn and Trish were putting the final touches to the table while singing a two-part tune, all the while watching the scene in front of them. The two families and grandparents had become as one. Patricia's parents were still a bit uncomfortable with this outdoor get-together, but at least they were trying.

Margaret did relax and join in more enthusiastically when she saw Klaus enjoying himself with John and Ethan. When the meal was ready they called the family together. Giggling children ran past as they made their way to wash up.

"Okay, time out you two." Ethan said, stopping in mid-swing and letting the horseshoe drop to the ground. "The ladies are calling for dinner."

Klaus said, "Just remember, I've been playing this game longer than both of you. I might ease up on you a bit after dinner." John and Ethan rolled their eyes and chuckled as all three were determined to win by nightfall. Klaus followed behind them, sporting a smile of contentment.

After settling at the table for the dinner prayer, everyone talked and laughed as they ate the delicious dinner. The children it seemed, hadn't eaten in days; their stomachs were bottomless.The men were ravenous from their games of horseshoes.

≈

The family continued to blossom. In 1881, Stephen Ray was welcomed with pride by all. Robert completed the McDougal clan in 1885.

Upon hearing of Robert's arrival, Jasper returned and bought land connected to John and Patricia's. He had been living in Kentucky and had never married. Jasper remained with them and became an even closer member of the family. He also resumed his employment with Mr. Heifelmeyer.

Chapter 14

The War Is Not Over

Jacob was also neutral—refusing to take part in someone else's war—as were John and Patricia. He was thirty years old, stood tall as an oak, and was well built. Jacob's chin was pointed, his face thin. He had a high brow. Jacob's hair was dark brown and kinky. His nose was straight, his lineage white and Indian. His voice naturally boomed. Jacob had creases in his forehead from frowning too much and creases at his mouth from smiling. His skin was leathery. His hands and feet were big. He was polite and limber. He could run like the wind. Jacob walked slowly. Once he was overheard telling John, "Why waste energy getting to a job?"

Both John and Klaus were in Pinkerton's National Detective Agency but were unaware of that fact when they first met. As an integral part of Pinkerton's National Detective Agency, both Klaus and John had Pinkerton's ear and trust. He knew the pulse of the nation.

Pinkerton and his sons after him were the unofficial head of law enforcement, i.e., sheriff, marshal, etc. Patricia's father had friends who worked for Pinkerton and were high up in the organization. Allan Pinkerton had his eyes on John for over a year before bringing him into the organization. John was one to talk, to let his feelings be known wherever he was, even the corner drinking establishment. This included his admiration for the President and Mr. Pinkerton.

John had a fantastic memory. He worked alone, staying in the gathering place for the President's Neutralists when necessary. He was not really " a spy," per se, but an " information- gatherer". He went from town to town asking questions discreetly. He had two different IDs.

A new type of seed was being developed, and John was asked to help. They were going to specialize in crop farming. Klaus and John merged the horse farm. There were horses on the farm, but that was not its real purpose. Seed was a code name for a new idea concerning the slaves.

Jacob was the main source for the horse farm and "seed." Most children on estate were Jacob's, one of the few favored farmhands. Two out of three women had children with him. He also had Pinkerton's ear and trust. He had almost as much influence as John did. Pinkerton looked up to

Jacob because he was educated and a free thinker, both of which were highly unusual for a person of Jacob's stature in the community.

Chapter 15

The Final Chapter

It was the summer of 1888, and Trish McDougal was enjoying the sounds of her children in the yard, chasing each other, giggling and shrieking with laughter. The cooling breezes danced around them. Trish chuckled at the antics of the children. *What a wonderful day*, she thought, one of the most beautiful she had seen. As always, her thoughts drifted to John. She could feel his love for her.

John had just returned from a mission. She had missed him so, even after twenty-one years of marriage. Trish found father and son working together not far away. She called to them and John looked up smiling at her. She continued walking toward her love, the father of her children. That little voice in her head suddenly screamed, "Run!"

She didn't reach him in time. As she picked John up, she saw the acknowledgment of what was happening in his eyes. As Trish gathered her beloved in her arms, Johnny realized what had just happened. She sat on the ground holding John and crooning to him as his life's-blood spilled onto her dress. John reached for her, gently touching her chin. "This is not goodbye, love."

Trish wasn't aware of his leaving. It was as if she were under a spell. She continued to cradle and sing was breathless as he returned with their neighbors, Ethan and Lynn Kilkesen, his parents' best friends. "Mother," Johnny kept repeating, as he knelt by her side, trying to get Trish's attention. He looked up helplessly at their neighbors.

Lynn eased Trish to her feet and took her and the children back into the house. Jacob helped them inside. Trish only made it as far as the settee before collapsing. Doc was summoned to tend to Trish. There was nothing to be done for John; he had been fatally wounded by a young man riding swiftly by. Patricia's parents were also called. Once Jacob was sure they were all in good hands with Lynn, he left to attend to his good friend John.

Outside, Jacob and Ethan lifted John's lifeless body into the wagon. Johnny accompanied the others on the trip into town; it was a very silent ride. After returning from town, Johnny almost collapsed as he sat down by the tree Becky, Stephen Ray, and young Robert had been chasing each other around only hours before. *They were laughing and frolicking right here, only a short time ago,* he thought. Now he could hear them, inconsolable, calling for their papa.

With arms wrapped tightly around his knees, he lowered his head and began to mourn. After a while, he raised his head and put much effort into composing himself. I must be strong for Mother and the others. I must take care of them. Rising slowly, he walked toward the door.

Trish's parents arrived shortly behind Doc. All three entered the house together. Doc immediately went about tending to Patricia, who was now in bed. He administered laudanum and offered his support. Patricia's parents walked in to see a whirlwind of activity. The younger grandchildren were sobbing, wanting their parents, asking where their big brother Johnny had gone with Ethan. Lynn was attempting to comfort the children. Together, Patricia's parents helped Lynn settle the children down.

Upon glancing at Patricia, Klaus became distraught and had to step outside for a moment. Instinctively, Margaret set about running the home, unsure what comfort she could offer her daughter. The feelings welling up in both Margaret and Klaus were foreign. They had always known the correct way to act, but this? They were completely at a loss for the proper response to this situation.

Seeing the state of Patricia's parents, Lynn also instinctively placed her hand on Margaret's shoulder, asking if she was all right. Margaret turned, hugged her, and asked if she could stay with them. Margaret saw how good Lynn was with the children and knew that she would need help not only with the children but with Patricia.

Officially, John was taken to the hospital for four days. In reality, he died and was buried in three days. Patricia's father had identified John's body. Patricia was unable to attend the viewing or burial. Word was sent from house to house that John had been murdered and that the culprit or culprits had escaped.

The undertaker cleaned John's wounds and prepared his body for the viewing. Gently, respectfully, the funeral director placed John in the gathering room of the couple's home and went about completing the final preparations for the viewing. Patricia was in no shape to receive anyone; she was out of her mind with grief.

John did not know his killer personally but knew of him. His death was made to look like an accident, but it wasn't. Both North and South were involved in

John's death. Each thought John was working for the other. There was still much distrust from both the North and South.

John was killed because of his work. Unofficially, word was sent out six months earlier for his capture. Powerful men in the government wanted John dead.

If John hadn't been killed he would have been hung for his "crime." John's only crime was working closely with the President and Pinkerton.

Big Tom was one of the men responsible for John's death. He was heard boasting of the murder in a roadhouse shortly after. Big Tom didn't get his name from his stature but because he talked so much. Many heard him boasting about a murder.

Jacob vowed to avenge John's death, and he would also be the one to look after John's family. Jacob had always been observant of those around him. He would remember even the smallest detail that most others would dismiss without thinking. His ability to observe others was heightened by John's death. Jacob could go into any roadhouse within fifty miles of his home. No one refused him entrance, possibly because of his size or the fear he inspired.

Big Tom and Jayme Duncan were found dead on the trail. It appeared that their horses had been startled and they were thrown, hit their heads on rocks and had broken their necks. There was little to no investigation into the deaths because the law had heard rumors of Big Tom's boasting.

The men Jacob killed to avenge John's death opposed the President's ideas of abolishing slavery. They were two large plantation owners from Virginia. Both were involved in the plot to kill John. William McPhearson was the mastermind of the plot and had over one hundred acres of land. George Wilson had less land than McPhearson. Wilson took four men from his plantation, young Billy McPhearson, and another man from the McPhearson plantation to carry out the murder.

After John's murder, William McPhearson was bold enough to leave his Virginia plantation and come to Louisiana with a plan to possess John's land, to add insult to injury.

Billy Richmond was found on a farm road leading from his property to the main road. His neck was broken. He was found on his back with his right leg bent. A farmhand found him because his horse came back without him. Everyone was shocked that he had been thrown from his mount, because it was the gentlest horse on the farm.

112

Robert Brown was found lying in the bushes on the side of the main road, about two miles from town. Some thought it looked like a robbery. His throat was cut from ear to ear, and his pockets were turned inside out.

Joey Hunter's was the goriest scene; he was beaten to death. His horse was next to him with a broken leg and had to be destroyed. There was blood on the horse's front right hoof. Everyone thought Joey had been trampled to death by his horse.

Jacob was found two days after Joey Hunter, alive but with dried blood on his head and bloody hands. One of the farmhands went over to wake Jacob, because he was normally an early riser. No one ever asked Jacob why he was covered with blood.

He killed seven men to exact revenge for John's death over a period of three years. Included in the seven were two high-ranking officials from the North. Each time someone was found dead, Jacob had been gone from the farm for a couple of days. Of the four men from the Wilson plantation, only three made it back to Virginia. No one knew who committed these crimes but Patricia. Jacob told her, "John can rest in peace now."

Afterword

What happened next? Look for the answers in Today, Tomorrow and Always – the family's continuing story. Grandpa Heifelmeyer takes Johnny into his confidence and under his wing. Johnny learns about events that his grandfather has attended that have become a part of American history.

Patricia is left alone with six children to raise in a time when that is not foreseen. Will Patricia find love again for herself and for the children?

FICTION

Forever and Always tells of the ups and downs of the freshly discovered love of a young couple, Patricia Heifelmeyer and John McDougal, at the end of the Civil War. The location of the book is Orleans Parish, the year of our Lord 1864. The war was almost over.

By now, the entire eating area of the cabin was engulfed in flames, which were quickly making their way to the door. If they didn't get out soon, there would be no chance of escape. Sparks flew everywhere; the heat was intense, the smoke blinding.

"We can do it, Johnny," Trish said reassuringly, hoping that he didn't hear the terror in her voice. Holding the twins tightly, covering their faces with a blanket from the bed, the four of them began their walk of terror through the fiery cabin to the safety awaiting them outside. John didn't have to be told to hold on to his mother's skirt; he wasn't about to let go. Slowly, carefully, they walked the thin path to safety.

Love, laughter, learning, mystery, secrecy, and murder are all woven throughout the pages of this book. The American Civil War raged from 1861 until 1865 and claimed more than 600,000 lives. Is John McDougal among their number?

Author Bio

CHRISTY SMITH turned her lifelong passion of writing into a career. Ever since childhood, Christy has always had pencil and notebook close-by to record her thoughts or sketch something. Her other interests include singing, reading and the art of crochet she learned from her grandmother as a child. She lends a helping hand to others whenever she can. Christy lives in a suburb of St. Louis, Missouri with her husband Jerry and their three cats. Their two grown children and four grandchildren live close-by.